THE
ROLY-POLY
SPIDER

THE ROLY-POLY SPIDER

by Jill Sardegna
Illustrated by Tedd Arnold

SCHOLASTIC INC.
New York Toronto London Auckland Sydney

With love to Heidi, Ross, and Jackie
—J.S.

For Ben and Leah
— T.A.

ISBN 0-590-84389-3

Text copyright © 1994 by Jill Sardegna.
Illustrations copyright © 1994 by Tedd Arnold.
All rights reserved. Published by Scholastic Inc.

12 11 10 9 8 7 6 5 4 3 2 1   2   6 7 8 9/9 01/0

Printed in the U.S.A.   23

Mr. Arnold used watercolor paints and colored pencils
to prepare the artwork for this book.

The roly-poly spider once spun a sticky web,

spun a sticky chair,
two couches and a bed.
"Come visit me," she cried,
"I'm as lonely as can be."

But the roly-poly spider was hungry, too —
you'll see.

The roly-poly spider was casting out a line;
she hooked a spotted beetle and reeled him in to dine.

"Sorry," said the beetle, "I really shouldn't stay."

But the roly-poly spider
drank beetle juice that day.

The roly-poly spider
spun on the garden lane.
She snagged a caterpillar
and asked him, "What's your name?"
He said, "My name is Lester.
I'm as handsome as can be."

Said the roly-poly spider,
"You look like lunch to me."

The roly-poly spider soon caught a bumblebee.
But he was fighting mad, so she waited patiently.
The more he fought, the more he stuck,
the more she smiled with glee.

And the roly-poly spider
had bee's knees with her tea.

The roly-poly spider set out a picnic treat.
Up jumped a ladybug, who stopped to talk and eat.
The time grew late; the treat was gone;
she wanted to be fed.

So the roly-poly spider
ate up her friend instead!

The roly-poly spider tossed out a silken thread.

Missed a skeeter's wing

and missed a sow bug's head.

At last her sticky noose roped in a great big fly.

Said the roly-poly spider,
"You'll be my shoofly pie."

The roly-poly spider was starving for romance.
Along came a millipede, who asked her for a dance.
"I'll teach you how to spin if you step into my web."

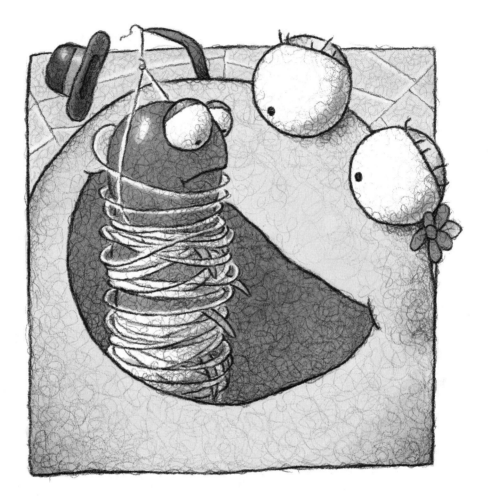

But the roly-poly spider spun him in her web instead.

The roly-poly spider went down a water spout.

But after all she ate, she was too fat to come out.
Stuck inside the middle, she was there to stay.

Said the roly-poly spider,
"I ate too much today."

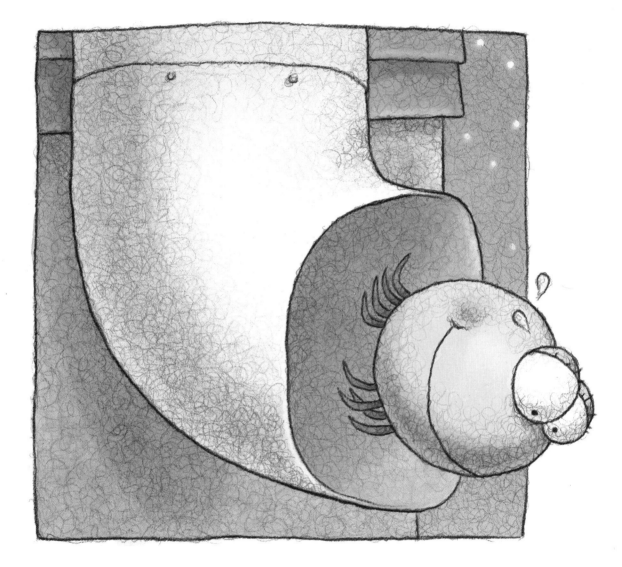

The roly-poly spider wriggled in the spout.
She wiggled and she wobbled till she finally popped out.

She looked up at the moon;
then she yawned and settled back.

Said the roly-poly spider,
"I need a bedtime snack!"